That Grand EASTER DAY!

WRITTEN BY
Jill Roman Lord

ILLUSTRATED BY Alessia Trunfio

Worthy kids
ideals®
Nashville, Tennessee

ISBN-13: 978-0-8249-5680-6

Published by WorthyKids/Ideals
An imprint of Worthy Publishing Group
A division of Worthy Media, Inc.
Nashville, Tennessee

Library of Congress Cataloging-in-Publication Data

Names: Lord, Jill Roman, author. | Trunfio, Alessia, illustrator.
Title: That grand Easter day! / Jill Roman Lord ; Alessia Trunfio.
Description: Nashville, Tennessee : WorthyKids/Ideals, [2018] | Summary:
    Illustrations and a cumulative rhyme reveal the events of Easter morning.
Identifiers: LCCN 2017030484 | ISBN 9780824956806 (hardcover : alk. paper)
Subjects: LCSH: Jesus Christ—Resurrection—Juvenile fiction. | CYAC: Stories
    in rhyme. | Jesus Christ—Resurrection—Fiction. | Easter—Fiction.
Classification: LCC PZ8.3.L877 Th 2018 | DDC [E]—dc23 LC record available
    at https://lccn.loc.gov/2017030484

Designed by Eve DeGrie

Printed and bound in China
RRD-SZ_Oct17_1

To Rebecca, Jamie, Megan, and Colby.
May Easter always be a grand event in your lives. —JRL.

To my mum, who inspires me with her faith. —AT.

"For God so loved the world
that he gave his one and only Son,
that whoever believes in him
shall not perish but have eternal life."

John 3:16

This is the place

where Jesus first lay

before he arose

on that grand Easter Day!

This is the stone

that blocked the way

that led to the place where Jesus first lay

before he arose on that grand Easter Day!

This is the man,

quite grumpy with gloom,
who stood with his sword in front of the tomb
and guarded the stone that blocked the way
that led to the place where Jesus first lay
before he arose on that grand Easter Day!

This is the bunny

that munched on a bloom
next to the man, quite grumpy with gloom,
who guarded the stone that blocked the way
that led to the place where Jesus first lay
before he arose on that grand Easter Day!

These are the ladies

with spice and perfume
to pour over Jesus, who lay in the tomb.

They strolled past the bunny
     that munched on a bloom
next to the man, quite grumpy with gloom,
who guarded the stone that blocked the way
that led to the place where Jesus first lay
before he arose on that grand Easter Day!

This is the angel

in radiant light

who said, "He's not here! There's no need for fright,"

to the ladies who carried their spice and perfume

but startled the man,
who fled with a zoom—
leaving the bunny that munched on a bloom
alone by the stone that was now rolled away,
revealing the place where Jesus first lay
before he arose on that grand Easter Day!

These are disciples

who heard the good news
then raced to the site with no time to lose,

but found the tomb empty—
   just linens as clues.
Gone was the angel
   who'd sat by the tomb
and spoke to the ladies
   with spice and perfume
but startled the man,
   who fled with a zoom—

leaving the bunny

    that munched on a bloom

alone by the stone that was now rolled away,

revealing the place where Jesus first lay

before he arose on that grand Easter Day!

This is Christ Jesus,

who gives life anew,

who rose up on Easter

for me and for you!

He left the tomb empty,

just linens as clues

found by disciples

who'd heard the good news.

Gone was the angel who'd sat by the tomb
and spoke to the ladies with spice and perfume
but startled the man, who fled with a zoom—
leaving the bunny that munched on a bloom
alone by the stone that was now rolled away,
revealing the place where Jesus first lay
before he arose on that grand Easter Day!

Christ Jesus arose

on that grand Easter Day!

"I have come
that they may have life,
and have it to the full."
John 10:10b